First published in 2018 in Great Britain by
Barrington Stoke Ltd
18 Walker Street, Edinburgh, EH3 7LP

www.barringtonstoke.co.uk

Text © 2018 Sita Brahmachari
Illustrations © Shutterstock.com

A CIP catalogue record for this book is available
from the British Library upon request

ISBN: 978-1-78112-696-7

Printed in China by Leo

The library is always... renfrewshirelibraries.co.uk

Visit now for
homework help
and free
eBooks.

SKOOBS

We are the Skoobs and we love the library!

Phone: 0300 300 1188
Email: libraries@renfrewshire.gov.uk

For my son Keshin – a singer songwriter and a soul man

And for the Zebra Crossing Man who saved Keshin's life when he was a boy

SIDE 1 ✳

TRACK 1: Hanger — 1

TRACK 2: Career — 15

TRACK 3: Pelican — 28

TRACK 4: Plot Your Journey Forward — 40

TRACK 5: Sky Shifting — 46

TRACK 6: Revision — 55

✳ SIDE 2

MEMORY TRACK 1: 'My Girl'
THE TEMPTATIONS — 64

MEMORY TRACK 2: 'Many Rivers To Cross'
JIMMY CLIFF — 70

MEMORY TRACK 3: 'Respect'
OTIS REDDING — 76

MEMORY TRACK 4: Jazz impro
CHARLES MINGUS — 83

MEMORY TRACK 5: 'Everything's Gonna Be Alright'
BOB MARLEY — 86

MEMORY TRACK 6: 'Happy Birthday'
STEVIE WONDER — 92

MEMORY TRACK 7: '(Sittin' On) The Dock of the Bay'
OTIS REDDING — 95

MEMORY TRACK 8: 'Everybody Hurts'
R.E.M. — 97

MEMORY TRACK 9: 'Sorry'
TRACY CHAPMAN — 100

MEMORY TRACK 10: 'Father and Son'
CAT STEVENS (YUSUF ISLAM) — 102

FUTURE SINGLE: 'Ferry Man'
OTIS LINDEN LAWRENCE & LENNY MARLON -114

Psychology exam -124

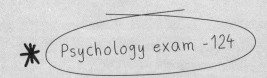

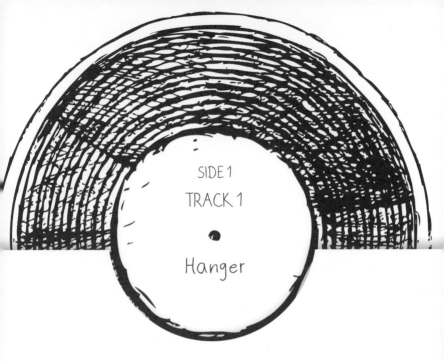

SIDE 1

TRACK 1

Hanger

I step out onto the road. There is time to cross, but it's tight. A woman in a flash red car is revving it up like she would run me over if she could. She waits till the very last moment to slam on her brakes so I'm forced to run the final few steps to the kerb.

She leans out of her tinted window and yells, "Why the hell don't you use the crossing?" Her cheeks are flushed and she's glowing redder by the second. She's nearly as red as her car now.

I saw this happen a couple of times when Otis was the zebra crossing man. Back when there still was a Zebra here.

That crossing's gone. They've replaced Otis and the Zebra he worked on with a Pelican! As if a few flashing lights could do what Otis used to –

Make me laugh.

Sing.

Teach me his music.

As if you can replace a Zebra with a Pelican. As if you can replace a human with a machine.

I mean, I know you can. Happens all the time.

It's like they think, 'What's the point of a person when a robot can do the job?'

But doesn't everyone know that you'll be missing something if you don't have a human at the crossing? Especially a one-off, one-of-a-kind human like Otis.

Even if he did lose it – that one time.

Am I starting to sound a bit like Otis?

I miss him on the crossing.

Most of all I miss his songs.

His velvet voice.

Him bending my ear.

Why couldn't they give him a second chance after all his zebra crossing years?

What did he call himself? "Me call me de healt' an' safety ferry man, makin' sure y'all safely cross this great big river of a road."

That final day ... It's not like he hurt anyone, and the mother decided not to take it further with the police.

Doesn't everybody deserve a second chance?

Even when he was still the Ferry Man.
His words used to lilt through my head
every day.
Just stuff like this.
He would say ...

"Man can learn a lat about hu-man nature right here on de crossin', Lenny ... It all about de way you cross ... all about de manner of crossin', Lenny son. Why else you t'ink I pass me life as a ferry man? It important work you know!"

Otis always spoke like he was just saying what he was saying, but I could always hear something deep running underneath – an undercurrent to the river of his words.

Otis was a crossing man
Otis was a ferry man
Otis was a river of thoughts
Otis was a river of words

When I was in primary school Otis explained why people like this red-face, red-car woman get so worked up when *they're* the ones in the wrong.

What Otis taught me on this road has
stuck in my mind
What Otis taught me on this road are
words that bind

He taught me to think of words like songs
in my head.
Otis was the best teacher I've ever had ...
And now school's ending
No island in the middle
Otis is gone
And I'm moving on
Otis was a crossing man
Otis was a ferry man

A car horn blasts me from my day dream back to the road. I'm about to stick the V-sign up at Red Car Woman, but stop myself as Otis's voice enters my head.

"Stay calm now, man. No waan get you'self all wound up ..."

No, that's not right. How did Otis say it? "All nyammed up ..."

"Over not'ing. It never wort' de aggro, Lenny son. Nat at all."

True! But *I* should be the angry one. I mean, *she* nearly knocks *me* over in her big chunk of red metal that could have seriously mashed me up. And here's me in my jeans and T-shirt, just some *body* with nothing to protect me.

Even when he was still on the crossing
His words used to lilt through my head
every day
Just stuff like this
He would say ...

"It all come from fear and hanger and a guilty con-shance. What is de point of gettin' up your blud pressure, man? All of we feelin' de pressure. So dem should jus' calm demself down an' stop wid de hanger!"

Otis said "anger" like "hanger" ... he added the "h" on purpose, enjoying his own "Otis lingo". He could say "anger" without the "h" – he just didn't choose to. I remember him saying ...

"These feelin's all mix up in *all of we* so dyam deep. When me was a yout' man me would get hangry if me didn't eat ... I would feed de hunger ... but now me get a likkle in-sight ... All kinda anger comes from hungry in one manner of t'inkin' or another, you nat agree, Lenny son? Hangry for love. Hangry for power. An' so many people jus' plain hangry for food."

*

I should have seen the build-up coming way before the day that Otis lost it.

But I see it now – how the hanger and the hunger grew day by day in Otis towards the end.

At least he left me his old record player and email address in case, "You waan come visit your old friend 'pon me paradise hisland ..."

But he left me no answer to why he lost it that day on the crossing ... and lost his job too, even if they dressed it up as "early retirement".

"Too much pressure in me blud buildin' on dis dyam road," Otis told me one morning. "Time to slow it down an' feel a likkle sunshine in me soul."

Now Red Car Woman is staring at me like she's waiting for *me* to say sorry.

I look up the road and I can hear the *beep, beep, beep* of the new Pelican as the road fills with people racing against the clock to get to school.

Children
Mums, Dads, Childminders
Prams, buggies
Scooters, heely-wheelies
Spokes of bike wheels turning, turning
All of them
Chatting on

Like nothing's changed
Like they're missing no one
Not missing Otis's smile
Not missing his laugh
Not missing his song
All of them
Chatting on
Like Otis isn't gone

A girl in a bright pink coat hits a bump as she
glides along in her heely-wheelies and trips up
half way across the Pelican. She flails one skinny
leg in the air, squeals and clings to her foot. But
now the lights are turning green. I catch the
look of panic on the mum's face as she parks her
buggy on the pavement, kicks the brakes on, and
turns back into the road to scoop up her kid.

Otis hated those wheelies.

His words lilt through my head every day
Just stuff like this
He would say ...

"Man! I am sick of dese new-fangle t'ings. Me can deal wid it as lang as me can see dem wheels. A bicycle is one t'ing, but a wheel on your heel to cross a road! What a way fe de world to turn!"

*

Now that I look back there were signs things weren't right in Otis's world. Otis was the calmest, most chilled person I knew, but sometimes I would see this look in his eye like he was proper afraid someone might get hurt on his Zebra. It was there in his eyes the day he saved my life.

"If only man could have be-hind sight – hindsight dem call it – de world would be a far, far better place. If only man could see what we see lookin' forward in place of lookin' back an' feelin' sorry. When it all too late to change ... too dyam late ..."

With *be-hind sight*, as Otis called it, there were signs, for sure. He'd say,

"I mus' be vig-i-lant, Lenny son. A ferry man mus' have eye in de back of him head"

My ears are still zinging with the girl's squeals on the Pelican.

If that was Otis's Zebra he would have been there holding up the traffic with his Lol –

Lolly Pop Stick
Striding out into the traffic
Stopping the mother's panic
Putting a smile on that little girl's face
Turning her screams to laughter with a joke
If Otis was here
He would have sung her a song
If Otis was here
She would not have been crying for so long

"It laugh out loud, don't you t'ink? Dat me – Otis Linden Lawrence – destined to be a music-al man, ended up on dis Zebra? After all me dreams of fame an' fortune, all me no-shuns fe singin' songs for de universe, crossin' dem rivers, crossin' dem roads. But hear me now, here me stand, a humble ferry man.

> Jus' crossin' over de road
> Jus' de road
> Getting by
> Singin' me road songs
> Singin' me soul songs
> In a manner of talkin'
> Here me stan', all de same
> With me Lol an' me Lenny son …
> Dat feelin' all right
> Nat everyt'ing gwaan be black an' white
> An' dat is Otis truth."

Why ever Otis stopped the traffic that day
Back before the summer holiday
Why ever he lost it
I can't say.

*

Red Car Woman is still staring at me.

"Can't you take your headphones off for just one moment?"

I pull them off and let them rest around my neck.

"What sort of example are you setting to those little ones?" She sticks out her hand and points her thumb back at the new Pelican. Now she jabs her finger at me. "You just walked out in front of me!"

I should say sorry. I must have shocked her, but the way she's yelling, there's no way *sorry* is coming out of my mouth.

"There used to be a zebra crossing here," I tell her.

She doesn't say anything. Just sits in her car ... waiting.

I hold both hands out, palms up, as if to ask, "What do you want me to say?"

She moves her hands to copy mine and gives me a pinched smile. "*I* don't see any markings!"

She's looking at me like I'm a fool.

No sign now of black and white
No island in the middle
No lights to cross at night
No sign of Otis
No gold-tooth smile
No glint in the eye
Every day
On my way
Every day
On my way home
No bad jokes
No good jokes
No songs
No high fives
No Otis philosophy
Psychology
No musings on "life an' de universe"
No putting the world to rights
No be-fore sight
No be-hind sight
No saving the day
No saving my life
No island in the middle, Lenny son
No island

"I asked you a question!" the woman snaps at me. "You nearly caused an accident."

Someone in a van beeps at her to move on. She mouths "Sorry!" into her mirror.

All polite
All contrite

"Idiot! You'll get yourself killed!" She revs her engine and accelerates away.

"Have a nice day!" I call after her.

Otis's words still lilt through my head
Every day
Just stuff like this
He would say ...

"Me nat hunderstand, Lenny son. Why dem so hangry dese days over some small-ish likkle t'ing. What is all dis rage about? Why caan't dem smile and wish you well? Whatever dem say I have only one t'ing fe answer like dem say in the U. S. of A. 'Have a nice day ...' me say. 'Have a nice day.'"

TRACK 2

Career

I suppose I am an idiot.

I must be.

I'm always getting lost in my random thoughts ... Otis called it 'Stream–of-con-shuss' song making. It flows like a river through my head, and maybe if I could think straight I wouldn't be re-taking my exams. If I'm not an idiot, why am I still here a year after all my friends have left?

Why am I slogging away – or *should* be – trying to get my third A Level?

I don't know why it's important any more. I don't know what I'm going to do next year, but – as David and Kwamé say – how can I know until I look about and see what's out there for me? And I suppose my dads are right.

Red writing sprawls across the noticeboard outside the hall. It looks like Mrs Wei's neat letters, but the sign's all wonky.

BIRTHPLACE OF
OPPORTUNITY

CAREERS FAIR!

I peer inside the hall. Maybe it *is* a joke.

It looks like the hall has always looked with a few display boards and long tables and a couple of sad helium balloons.

There are about twenty students, mostly from year 11, on chairs dotted around the hall. I never came here in year 11 … No matter how many times David and Kwamé ask I haven't got a clue what I'm going to do after A Levels, but there's plenty of people who do have ideas on my behalf.

Kwamé thinks I should do a music degree "for sure". *He* might be sure but *I* don't know. All that money in fees to pay back and money to find for somewhere to live ... and how will I do that if I'm playing in a band or busking?

I walk over to the empty "Apprenticeship" stand and scan it for anything about music. All I can find is a leaflet from an advertising agency which wants to recruit "creative young minds".

I am young
I am creative
I do have a mind

So maybe I am just about qualified for this.

I think about taking the leaflet when a man walks over. He's wearing a blue suit with the trouser lines ironed wonky.

"Interested in anything?" he asks.

"It's OK, thanks!" I say, and I drop the leaflet and move away.

And how am *I* the idiot?

Of course I'm interested in something.
Everyone's interested in something.
I just don't know what something!

I turn around and follow the walls of grey-white paint back to the door. I reckon I might have nightmares tonight about being stuck for ever in this hall. The last time I was here was for my mock exams, and I have this swilling in my gut that I get whenever I sit down to an exam. It feels like any work I've done has drained out of me and is pouring into someone else's pen instead.

I can't believe that in a few weeks' time I will come in here again and sit at one of the desks lined up in military rows. Since year 9 I've had to jam my legs under them, which makes me feel like a giant in a world made for kids.

My legs jangle with nerves when I think about my final shot at the Psychology exam. It feels like I've been doing my A Levels for five years not three.

"*No more second chances,*" David told me. "*You've got to pass it this time around.*"

Thanks, Dad!

"*Three solid A Levels is what you need.*"

I don't know how many times David thinks he has to say that. Even if I am an idiot, his message has sunk in all right.

Psychology
Music
Media Studies

And to think ... back when I chose these three subjects everyone thought they were too easy for me!

"*Not serious enough!*" David came right out and said what he thought, as usual.

I know Kwamé was thinking it too.

It came as a bit of shock for me. I sort of thought A Levels were like GCSEs ... you could just turn up in class and then wing the exams. That was back then. I haven't wasted a whole year hanging around this place while all my mates have moved on for nothing.

*

Why do these Year 11 kids look so keen?

Why do I never feel like that, apart from when I'm writing my songs?

I don't get it. How can you decide what to do when you haven't really done anything yet?

I glance around the hall. Now I look closer, as well as the sad balloons there are little flags dotted around to advertise careers in –

Health
Law
Banking / Finance
Police
Leisure Services
Civil Service
Care Services
Transport

There's only one table free from students. A police officer is sitting on her own at it. She doesn't look much older than me. She's like a Year 11 girl in fancy dress!

I must be staring at her because she looks up and smiles, and as soon as she does I know her.

"Naira!" I call out. I haven't said her name in ages.

In fact, I haven't seen her in years.

I check out her name badge. I'm right. No one could forget Naira's green eyes!

"Hi," she says. She looks a bit freaked out.

"It's Lenny," I say. "Our parents used to hang out together when we were in primary."

Naira stares at me for a bit longer and then it dawns on her.

"Little Len!"

I draw myself up to my full six foot two. "Less of the little, thanks!"

It's weird remembering someone from when you were a kid, before you had any of *these* "dyam feelin's" as Otis would say. And now seeing that same girl – woman – again and thinking … things I shouldn't be thinking.

This is too awkward.

Naira must be reading my mind because she blushes up and she starts to tidy leaflets away.

Mrs Wei slides past me and says, "Good to see you here, Lenny. Don't forget our tutorial on Friday, will you?"

Then Mrs Wei leans in and whispers, "I didn't know you had an interest in the police, Lenny."

"I haven't."

"Well, we *should* all keep an open mind!" Mrs Wei says as she raises her eyebrows to Naira.

"Always!" I laugh.

I'll miss joking around with Mrs Wei when I've left. She sighs at me for going off on tracks of random thoughts, but we know each other pretty well and I think she'll miss me too.

"Go on, Len," Naira says. "I'm still training so I need the practice." She taps the table for me to sit down.

I sit and pull my chair in. My foot clips Naira's and she moves her legs to the side.

"Do me a favour and pretend you're a bit interested, will you?" Naira says.

"I am," I tell her with a laugh.

"Why don't you try this test?" she says, ignoring my attempt at flirting. "You can be my first guinea pig."

"Thanks … I think!" I say. "All right. What do I have to do?"

I can't help looking into her eyes. They're shot through with hazel, green and flecks of gold – a globe of spinning colour.

"The test is quite interesting," Naira tells me. "And you did recognise me from when we were kids, so maybe you are –"

I have no idea what she's talking about. "Sorry! Maybe I am *what?*"

"A super-recogniser."

It sounds a bit unlikely. Super's not really me.

Super intelligent – (Not)

Superman – (Not in any ripped way – not last time I looked in the mirror – but right now I wish I was!)

Supersonic – (Not fast at all! I can hardly cross the road without getting flattened.)

"What's a super-recogniser?" I ask.

Naira pushes a photo of a crowd of people across the table. "You've got to study the faces for three minutes," she tells me.

She sets a stopwatch. I glance up at her. I can't get over how sorted she looks.

I'm looking at the faces and thinking ...

How do you get to be that sorted so young? She's only three years older than me, but Naira seems to have done a fast-forward flip into the future that I can't even imagine.

The timer goes off. Then Naira takes the photo away and starts chatting to me.

"So how's the family?" she asks.

"They're good. Yours?"

"Split up last year."

"Sorry to hear that," I say.

"Thanks, Len. It's been tough. But ... they're friends and everything." Naira shrugs and checks her watch.

I feel like she's only talking to fill time. Maybe I'm boring her.

"I have to distract you for five minutes," she explains. "I'm meant to talk about something different to make you forget what you've been looking at."

I can't help looking at Naira's mouth as she talks. She doesn't need to try to distract me! Is it wrong of me to flirt with her? I mean, we did know each other as kids and she's only a *bit* older than me …

"Earth to Len!" Naira laughs. She used to say that all the time. She taps the table. "OK, you can focus again now."

"I'm not so great at the focus bit," I tell her.

Naira produces a box of passport-style photos and lays them all out. I recognise some of the faces right away, but there are loads of them. Loads more faces than were in the group shot. "So which of these people did you spot in the crowd?" she asks.

There's a couple of faces I recognise and there's two others I think might have been there. The rest I know I've never seen before.

I study them for a while longer. There are two men with Rasta locks. One of them looks a bit like Otis when he was younger. I try to scan the crowd photo from memory left to right, left to right … I'm pretty sure now the man who looks like Otis wasn't in the crowd – I've just got Otis on my mind – so I rule him out and take that photo out.

"I think that's everyone," I say, and I push the line-up of faces over to Naira.

"And that's your final choice?" she asks, as if she's a game show host.

I play along and do a *tick-tock, tick-tock* countdown.

"My final choice!" I declare.

Naira brings out the crowd photo.

"Congratulations," she says. "You'd have to do more tests, but if you're interested you could be a candidate for the new Super-Recogniser Team."

"Serious?" I ask.

"Serious! There's this whole new unit and you could be part of it."

"Part of what?"

"Surveillance," Naira explains. "You'd learn how to spot faces in a crowd, check out people up to no good!"

"Nah!" I shake my head. "That's not for me."

"OK, but can I *say* you're interested?" Naira asks and puts my form in a box labelled

Interested Candidates. "At least it won't *look* like I've wasted my time."

I shrug. "OK."

"What *are* you into then, Len?"

"No idea," I tell her. But I *am* into how she calls me Len.

Then I look down at the face of the man who has a smile like Otis's and say, "I'm into music. I write songs ..."

"Oh yeah," she says. "I remember when you got your guitar. Have you recorded anything I can listen to?"

"Got a few up on SoundCloud, but who hasn't? I don't know what I'm gonna do, to be honest ... Maybe I'll be a zebra crossing man!"

"Random as ever," Naira says and grins. "If you ask me, I think that would be a waste ... Oh sorry, Len!" Naira looks past me. "Seems like I've got a bit of queue."

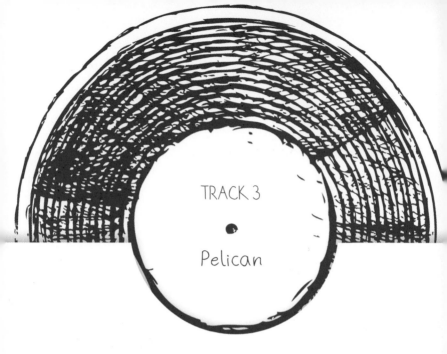

TRACK 3

Pelican

I pick my guitar off its stand and try out a few riffs then scribble some lines down in my notebook. A random drift of ideas floats through my head.

My crossing's gone
All painted over
All painted over now
Just press that button and walk

Walk, don't talk
Walk, don't talk
It's not the same.
It's a shame
That's all
No more crossing
No yellow light to get me through the night
No island in the middle
My crossing's gone
All painted over now
All painted over
No more crossing song
No more soul songs
It's not the same
It's a shame
That's all

I scrub most of the lines out and start again.
That's how it goes. I can fill up a whole notebook
working out one song and most of the time it
doesn't turn into anything … at best maybe I use
one line or a couple of words.

ZEBRA CROSSING SOUL SONG

Zebra Crossing Soul Songs?
Soul Song?
Soul Songs?
Rings in your ear. Too many S's.
Sometimes I just like the way the
    words sing in your mind
Soul Song …
I like the way the words sit there
All kind of innocent at first like they
    don't mean that much
Till you look into the way
They sway
Dey sway
They cross
Dem cross
Leap, buck
Fly across de page
Not like a pelican
Zebras can leap
Peli-cans — caan't

If I showed anyone my songwriting
notebooks they might seriously worry
about me ...

What's it all about
If black and white are painted out
No Island in the middle Otis man
No Island in the middle
After all this time
Of helping me across the road
Now all I see is people getting hangry
No Island in the middle Otis man
No Island in the middle

I met a girl today
Naira of the gold-green eyes
She used to hold my hand and cross
    with us
Back in the day
When we were kids
~~And everything was just for play~~ (Aaagh!)
And everything was still to play.

"What's this?" Kwamé asks as he comes in. He takes off his jacket and checks out my notebook.

I move it out of his sight. "Nothing!" I say. "Just some words I was messing about with."

"Not revision then?"

"This is for Otis," I say.

"Have you heard from him?" Kwamé sighs. "Poor old Otis. Is he any better?"

"Says he's loving it with his sister. Starting to chill. Sunning himself."

"Sittin' by the St Lu-shan sea!
Sunnin' meself and gettin' me a big fat belly
From lyin' around, kickin' up de sand
In place of standin' all day in de road
Nat as active as me used to be
When me was de Ferry Man."

"That's Otis all right!" Kwamé laughs. "It's a shame he had to leave like that. Feels like we should have thrown him a street party as a send-off. But he's well out of here. That grimy road for a St Lucian beach! I know what I would choose."

"I don't think he had much choice," I say.

"I know, Len. You really miss him?"

I nod.

"Me too." Kwamé shakes his head. "The road's not the same without him."

"But you and David didn't even like him at first …" I think out loud.

"At first," Kwamé admits. "And we didn't think he liked *us* much, the way he looked at me and David together … like he didn't approve. But after all those years of crossing I suppose he got us and we got him. We all grew on each other in the end." Kwamé picks up a photo of me in nursery and does one of his 'bless' looks. "He saved your life! You don't forget something like that."

Then Kwamé peers at my notebook again and tries to read my lyrics.

"Who's the girl with the gold-green eyes?" he teases.

"*None* of your business!"

Kwamé shrugs and heads for the kitchen.

The front door opens and David is in the hall.

"How did the careers thing go?" David comes in and ruffles my hair.

"Dad!" I ruffle it back. "How would you like it if I did that to you?"

He smooths his hand over his shiny head and grins. "I should be so lucky! So how did the careers thing go?"

"OK," I say. "I did a test. Seems like I'm a Super-Recogniser!"

"Impressive," David says, but he doesn't sound so sure.

"Remember Naira?" I ask. "You were friends with her mums in primary school."

Kwamé comes and stands in the kitchen doorway. "Yeah! I remember," he says.

"Well, she's a trainee police officer now – and she tested me on ..."

"Beautiful Naira – a police officer!" David interrupts.

I do my best not to look awkward. I wish these two didn't have such good radars for when

I fancy someone. If I've got super-recogniser powers, I know where they came from!

I'm half way into describing the test when Kwamé hijacks our chat with a trip down memory lane of all the stuff he did with Colette, one of Naira's mums, when they were on the fundraising committee at our primary school.

"What was the name of Naira's other mum?" Kwamé asks.

"No idea," David says. I can tell he's not that interested.

"I didn't *actually* expect you to remember," Kwamé chips in.

I hope they're not going to start bickering.

"What's that supposed to mean?" David asks. He's got a smile on his face, but that doesn't count for anything.

"I just mean, you wouldn't remember because it was mostly me –"

"I did my bit!" David protests.

"Let's see!" Kwamé starts finger-counting. "Twenty-six bake sales, three school discos, seven Summer Fairs ... oh and DJing one truly historic

Bollywood dance night! And let's not forget the six Burns suppers."

"Hang on," says David. "Remember those Burns Night speeches? It always took me ages to rehearse ..." David tilts his chin in the air, arms up conducting, as he switches into performance mode.

"*Then gently scan your brother man.*" David turns up the volume on his Scottish accent as he recites a Robert Burns poem –

*"Still gentler sister woman
Tho' they may gang a kennin wrang
To step aside is human."*

"OK, OK ... step aside, brother man!" Kwamé says. "You know I can never resist your Rabbie Burns!" Kwamé grins at his own lame attempt at a Scottish accent.

I can't help but laugh as the two of them smooch around like they've got their own secret sound track in their heads. "Get a room!"

"How about we have a reunion with Colette and what's-her-name?" Kwamé says.

"See, *you* don't remember her name either," David replies.

"Don't bother," I tell them. "They're not together any more."

The news that Naira's mums have split up sends David and Kwamé off on an even bigger nostalgia trip. To be honest, I could do without it.

I try to blur their voices out and carry on with my song ... but it's no good.

"Makes you realise we've done OK!" Kwamé says to David.

"So what jobs can you do when you're a super-recogniser?" David asks as he sits next to me.

"Join the police," I say. "Be a spy ... surveillance."

"Maybe not!" David says. "So what else did they suggest for you, Mr Bond?"

"They didn't!" I keep on writing.

The sound track of my mind right now is 'Many Rivers To Cross'. It's the first song Otis taught me and it might still be my favourite.

"Yu caan't beat a riff from me man Jimmy Cliff."

Otis's words lilt through my head
Every day
Just stuff like this
He would sing-say ...

"Listen up now, man, if you waan be a musi-shan
Tek a lyric down
Catch dem word dat hinspire
Listen deep inside de music
See what plays thru ya
See what plays true to ya
You gotta search for a song that sings thru ya, t'ru an' true"

Search for a song that sings true ...

He understood about song-say ... sing-say.

He understood how to make a song say something.

Otis.

I met a girl today
Someone I knew yesterday
From a time of childhood
Play
That was way back in the day
But I still can't find my way

Naira of the green eyes
Naira of the gold-green eyes
Naira of the green eyes

No one could forget
But meeting her was nothing like back in
the day
When we were kids
And everything was still fe play.
That was way back in the day
But I still can't find my way.

TRACK 4

Plot Your Journey Forward

That's it with school now. We're off timetable for revision.

Well ... except for Mrs Wei's tutorials.

Revision is what I should have been doing since the Careers Fair. But I can't stop thinking about Otis ... and Naira.

And trying to make sense of the mash-up that is my head.

How did I manage to let all this time glide by?

"Time is not a vortex for you to disappear down, Len!" That's one of David's favourite sayings. Perhaps he thinks it's poetic.

Seems like David's wrong. Time *is* a vortex, a space–time continuum that I live inside. I've been floating around in it … probably for ever!

That's how come it's Friday already – my tutorial day.

Today I have to tell Mrs Wei what my plans are for after A Levels.

Today I have to tell Mrs Wei what revision I've done … or not done.

Today I have to tell Mrs Wei that she might as well pray for me, like she says she does sometimes, because I haven't got as far as I was meant to.

After last time, it's fair enough that she keeps tabs on me. She says it's the college's responsibility to "plot each student's journey forward" – whatever that means.

The other day, I reminded David about what Otis said after I failed Psychology the first time. I didn't mean to, but Otis's words reeled right out of my head and into my mouth. It was a big mistake.

"You jus' con-cen-trate dat mind on writin' dem songs, Lenny son, travel some an' give dat

talent a likkle road trip! Do some growin' up fe you'self and den you can mek up your mind. When you get as old as Otis you got plenty, plenty time for be-hind sight … We caan't all be as lightnin' flash as that Usain Bolt. For most of we, Life is not'ing like a sprint, son! Faster you learn that, faster you start winnin'."

*

I get why my dads think there are better people to give me careers advice than Otis, but his words helped me back then. I still think what David said was harsh.

"So," David said, his voice cold with disappointment, after I told him my results and let slip Otis's take on life. "You think it's a good idea to take advice off a part-time busker, part-time zebra crossing man who's full-time lost his way?"

True, I don't know what went on for Otis that day on the crossing, but David's wrong about Otis's advice. He's taught me loads. I don't care what anyone says, some of the best stuff I've got, I got from Otis.

These are the mashed-up thoughts sprinting round my head as I press the button at the Pelican on my way to my tutorial.

I'm off today
To weigh my future
With Mrs Wei
Everything is in the balance
Why do I even bother?

Plot your journey forward
Feel no doubt
Just close your eyes and cross the road
Plot your journey forward
Feel no doubt
Just stop asking what it's all about
Walk, don't talk
Walk, don't talk
Don't talk
Just walk!
Don't think
Don't blink

'Did I have to wait this long till the traffic stopped last time?' I wonder.

A woman on the other side of the pavement calls out to me.

"It's broken, love! Didn't last long, did it? They're coming to fix it later."

Is that the title of a song – 'Broken Love'? If it isn't it should be.

How unfair is this? The Pelican gets a second chance, but Otis didn't.

I stand on the pavement and try to think back to when I first heard David reciting Rabbie Burns. In my mind's ear, David's in full flow.

"Then gently scan your brother man
Still gentler sister woman
Tho' they may gang a kennin wrang
To step aside is human."

Even when I was little, I loved the music of David's Scottish accent. I wished I had my own accent to slip into.

"What's *kennin*? What's the song mean?" I hear the voice of my five-year-old self as I listened to David practise his lines.

"*Kennin wrang* ... wrong thinking!" David said. He picked me up as he explained. "Rabbie Burns was a good soul. I'm no poet, but I think the words mean something like – be gentle with each other, because we all make mistakes ..." David said the lines again and then went on, "To make mistakes is human. Be kind to each other. Don't judge ..."

He was about to say more, but I started to squirm out of his arms.

"OK, I get it, Dad!" my little boy's voice says in my ear. "You can put me down now!"

I haven't really thought about this before, but I start to realise that maybe I didn't catch my rhyming from Otis. My search for the rhythm and rhyme of words must have started long before I met Otis.

TRACK 5

Sky Shifting

Mrs Wei's office just fits two comfy chairs and a low table. I have to edge around the table to sit down.

> *No leg room*
> *No escape*
> *Not even staring out of the window space*
> *Except for the sky*
> *light.*

The clouds pass fast above my head, like the sky's shifting. A plane flies low, its sound blasting the clouds. I track its path.

Mrs Wei sits down opposite me.

"No time for day dreams, Lenny!" she says as she follows my gaze. "Let's talk about careers progress first." She takes a sheet of paper off the table and waves it at me. "So, this report tells me you showed an interest in joining the police or security services." Mrs Wei doesn't look like she believes it.

I look back at her, my face blank. I think of Naira's eyes, bright with laughter. The chorus of her song is stuck in my head ...

Naira of the green eyes
Naira of the gold-green eyes
Naira of the green eyes
No one could forget

"Lenny?" Mrs Wei taps me on the arm.

"I did a test that's all," I say. "Turns out I'm a super-recogniser."

"Now that *is* interesting," Mrs Wei says. "I've always thought you had good visual recall. But how's the revision going?"

"Hard!" I tell her. *Hardly at all*, is what I don't say.

"You'll need to use your V.S.S."

"My what?"

"Just testing!" Mrs Wei says. "Come on, Lenny. Your Visual-Spatial Sketchpad."

"Oh, yeah. I remember now."

Mrs Wei got us to draw doodles to remind us to match an image with an idea to help us remember stuff better. I can even picture the doodles I did in the margins.

"That's a relief." Mrs Wei sighs. "Please, Lenny. Just put in the work for the exam. It's even more important this time, now there's less coursework. You deserve to do well. You're so observant about people – you're a natural at psychology."

"I'd do better this time if it was more coursework, like it used to be," I mumble.

"We can't do anything about that ..." Mrs Wei pulls a face like she's not happy about the changes either. "It means you need to study the theory in more depth than ever. Use all my tricks. Cover your notes in colour, draw pictures, link information with things that have happened to you. Remember ... what sticks is what you're connected to emotionally ... the people and situations you care about ... Do you recall our work on empathy?"

I don't. I feel sorry for Mrs Wei. She loves her subject and she so wants me to do well.

"Like what – things about empathy?" I ask.

"First day of school, birthdays ..." she says. "Does the term 'emotional investment' ring any bells?"

"Kind of."

"You're not filling me with confidence, Lenny. What topic are you revising at the moment?"

"Memory!" I say, which is the first thing that comes into my head. "I've been thinking about Otis. You know, who used to be the zebra crossing man."

"The one who caused that ..." Mrs Wei searches for the right word ... "incident?"

I nod.

Mrs Wei twists her mouth to one side like she does when I'm drifting but she wants to give me a chance to explain.

"I've known him since I was in nursery," I say. "I've been thinking about all the times I crossed at the zebra and all the memories ..."

"Yes!" Mrs Wei says, happier now. "That could work in an essay on episodic memory. On how the repeated action of crossing the road fixes your memory. Why not? Tell you what ... work on Memory for next Friday."

"But there's so much theory to learn," I say with a groan.

"Well, let's learn it then. Break it all down into chunks like I showed you. You could write down your memories, then explore a theory that links to what you've written."

From Mrs Wei's face, I guess I must be frowning.

"Don't look so worried, Lenny," she says. "In our next tutorial I'll help you match the memories to the theory. It'll be worth it ... Memory almost always comes up in the exam." Mrs Wei looks at her iPad to check she's covered everything. "Now, I've prepared you a revision timetable."

Mrs Wei prints off two sheets and hands them to me. "Plenty for you here, Lenny."

I go to stand up, but I tip the table and have to sit back down to steady it.

"We're not finished yet," Mrs Wei says. "Am I right in thinking you still haven't applied to do anything after your results?"

I sink into my seat.

"I thought not." Mrs Wei sighs like she would prefer not to be right about this. "So what shall I put down here for you?"

"Put ... I'm going to work for a bit and get the money together to go travelling."

"There isn't a tick box for that!" Mrs Wei jokes. "Where do you plan to go?"

"I haven't decided, but my parents say if I work hard they'll help me pay for a flight to St Lucia."

"Well, there's an incentive. And if you want to travel and learn at the same time ..." Mrs Wei hands me some V.S.O. leaflets. "Have a think about volunteering. You'd have a lot to offer, Lenny."

*

I press the button on the Pelican, but no lights come on and a constant flow of traffic streams up the road.

I read the leaflets while I wait. One of the V.S.O. projects is in Malawi – they want musicians with "the ability to sing, write and play songs" to help teach English. Maybe there *are* things I can do.

The Pelican still isn't working, but a car pulls up at the kerb. I recognise the wing mirrors – in an odd position half way down the bonnet. Music's blaring out of the window. It's that charity version of 'A Bridge Over Troubled Water' as it builds to the chorus. The choir swells the road. And my heart swells with it.

"I heard from Otis today," Maeve calls out from the driver's seat of her Triumph Herald. "He says he's started singing again. I'm still waiting for my invite to play in our old band. Who knows? I may yet get a Caribbean tour!"

I catch that teasing spark of humour in her eyes and remember how she used to flirt with

Otis. I used to think Maeve was a bit in love with Otis, but *he* never seemed *that* interested.

"Yeah, sounds like he's doing all right," I shout back.

The car behind Maeve's beeps its horn and swerves around the old Triumph.

"Keep your cool, honey pie," she calls out.

"Why is everyone so hangry, hangry, hangry
Don't they know it's all about de crossin',
crossin'
All about de crossin' songs ..."

Maeve waits for me to cross the road then drives on over where the zebra stripes used to be at the speed of a snail. It's like she's on a go-slow in honour of Otis.

I watch the Herald chug down the road, the mirrors sticking out like over-sized ears. I could catch up with Maeve and ask her what she knows about Otis. Maybe then I could work out what happened, but while I'm thinking about it she turns the corner and is gone.

I wonder how many people will really miss Otis? Probably more than I know. But how can you truly miss someone when all you know about them are the bits you've found out when you're crossing the road?

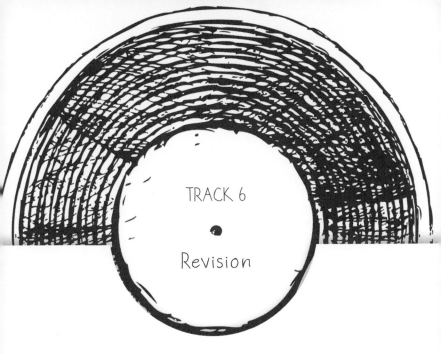

TRACK 6

Revision

I read the notes I took on Long-term Memory.

Nothing goes in.

I read over the same lines again and again, but the words float in front of my eyes. I wonder if there are any joined up pathways between my eyes and my brain. Maybe I've got some wires missing.

Memory
Three types
Procedural, semantic and episodic

Procedural = permanent memory — automatic — memory of how to ride a bike, swim, tie shoelaces, play guitar? Once you know how to do it, you always have that memory as long as you have the capacity to remember.

> What? Did this ever make sense to me?
> Maybe I just don't have the 'capacity'?

Semantic memory

Semantic = Store.

Remembering — storing up information, words — what you know for a fact. (Not much!)

Episodic memory

Episodic = Events that you'll remember strongly. Involves conscious thought.

I've scribbled something else in my notes ...

We might have a semantic memory for 'knowing that' Paris is the capital of France, and we might have an episodic memory for 'knowing that' we caught the bus today.

So, I think, that's like if I just know something's true? A kind of *kennin*, to use Rabbie Burns's word. But I might have got that *kennin wrang*.

This is what happens when I revise. I get to a point where it all makes sense, but only just ... like my understanding of it is hanging by a thread. Then a switch flicks and the understanding bit of the circuit cuts out, my head goes fuzzy and I give up.

What did Mrs Wei say about remembering things you care about?

There's lots about growing up I don't really remember. When David or Kwamé ask me, "Don't you remember the day ...?" lots of the time I can't remember much about the times they think are so important ... like their wedding. I'm not going to tell them this, but I don't remember it that well. I was only five. They've kept the tiny blue suit I wore as a memento – well, it *would* be a memento if I remembered wearing it. I guess it's a memento for them!

Now I'm 18, there are loads of things that I should have logged in my memory but haven't. It's like I have memory blanks, even when Kwamé shoves photos under my nose to prove I was there. "Look, Lenny. You *were* with us!"

But loads of what I do remember happened on the Zebra, as random as it might seem.

I overheard my dads talking about me last night.

Kwamé – "It's like since they painted out that zebra crossing, Lenny seems a bit lost."

David – "Or maybe he just misses Otis ..."

Kwamé's right. I *do* feel like someone's painted over a big part of my past.

After all, I've been going over those black and white lines most days of my life.

I grab my songbook and write.

All those times
Imprinted in my mind
All those times
In-printed on my mind.

Song Idea

All those times in-printed on my mind.
   Painted in before I started nursery.
Painted out at Easter after Otis's
   "retirement".
My memories from that road have been
   building up in me for 15 years.
Most of my life.

*

Question to Mrs Wei.

   Could the repetition of crossing to and from
school have sealed in the memories of Otis with
my memories of growing up?

   His words lilt through my head every day
   Just stuff like this
   He would sing-say ...

   "Startin' with Otis Redding ... me namesake ...
an' travellin' on a mus-i-cal adventure ..."

   "*Sittin' on the dock of the bay.*" Our voices
fuse together – me and Otis.

The crossing might have gone, but memories of the road, of growing up, still sing to me.

The road is singing ... with all the songs that Otis taught me on that crossing.

I take my guitar and start to strum.

*

David sticks his head around the door and holds his hand out for me to pass him my guitar.

"Come on, Len. You promised us you'd get on with your revision."

"I am!" I say, and I point my guitar at the psychology book open on the desk.

"Sounded like it!"

I shrug and pass him my guitar.

"Two hours' solid revision and I'll bring it back," David promises.

I pick up a pencil and scribble some notes about my memories of Otis, but I don't get very far. What I want to do is run outside like I used to after school and sit on the wall with Otis and talk. It feels so weird him leaving like that without telling me what was going on ...

Why?

Then an idea jumps into my head that might lead to an answer. What if I write to Otis and share my zebra crossing memories with him? Maybe then he'll find a way to tell me why he lost it that day and was forced to go away.

I push my notebook aside, flick open my laptop, click on Otis's email address and start to write.

Dear Otis,

I'm hoping you can help me out here. For my Psychology exam. You know I have to take it again. Well, my tutor's trying to find ways to help me keep stuff in my head. I've got to find some memories to talk about – based around "episodic memory". It sounds fancy, but it just means something you repeat often enough for the memory to print itself into you, so you never forget it.

Anyway, you know how you used to help me out by sitting on the wall and listening? Do you mind if I imagine you're back at the end of the road and we're sitting on that wall right now?

I've got to get this work done – somehow. So, even if I don't send this to you, it's one way of unscrambling my mind!

I'm playing your songs on your old record player while I write. Thanks again! Apart from my guitar it's the best present anyone's ever given me. In fact, those songs are helping me to work out how to structure things. I was stuck and then I started to line up the records in the order I remember you introduced me to them.

I like the whole ritual of handling the vinyl, blowing the fluff off the needle and finding the place where the track starts. I like picking the needle up to move the record on when it gets stuck in a scratch groove. It sort of moves me on too.

Thanks for inviting me to visit. I will
one day (if I can get the cash together),
but first, Otis ... I need to know what
happened. I need answers to the
questions written in these memory tracks.
(I'll attach them.)

I suppose that's what I wanted to say.
It's much easier to sit on a wall and talk
like we used to, watching the traffic pass
by, watching the river.

Oh, I know what I wanted to say.

Remember I told you about Naira? Well,
I did what you said and wrote a song
for her ... And Maeve says to say hello.
Watch out! She's waiting for her invite!

Chat soon.
Lenny

P.S. I've posted a new song on
SoundCloud.

I blow the fluff off the needle and rest it
gently in the groove ...

SIDE 2
MEMORY TRACK 1

'My Girl'
THE TEMPTATIONS

Music's a bit like smell, isn't it? Takes you right back there.

First day of school.

Fresh wet paint.

I'm four years old again.

I'm sitting on our step, sniffing the paint.

Kwamé wrinkles up his nose like he isn't sure he likes the smell.

"Don't breathe that in, Len," he says. "The car fumes are bad enough!"

But I like the smell.

I climb on my scooter.

Kwamé holds onto the handles because I can't ride it properly yet. He has to hunch over and run along with me as I coast down the hill to the new zebra crossing and the whiff of fresh paint.

You're there, Otis, waiting for us.

I don't know your name yet and you don't know mine.

I like your smile.

Your gold tooth glinting.

Rasta locks swaying over your long coat.

You're tall. As tall as Kwamé. You chat to him and ask him where he's from. Kwamé says, "Here! And my parents were from Nigeria."

And I ask Kwamé, "Where is Nigeria on the map of the universe?"

You start singing, a song about history ... and knowing where you come from. Then you look at me and smile.

"Now that's what I call one smart scooter-man!"

People are lining up along the pavement waiting to cross and you're waving your hands around like a conductor. You look like you're about to dance us across the road.

"I waan hapologise on behalf of de art'orities. It suppose' to be a safety crossin' not an hobsti-cal course! De wet paint will stick to dem likkle feet. De black is dry up so me hadvise you to leap over de white like dis!"

Then you jump over the white lines onto the black to show us how to cross.

"Like a herd of zebras, buckin' and leapin' now I t'ink of it. Dat be de way to get to school!"

You fling back your locks and laugh.

"Why is his hair so long?" I ask Kwamé. "It looks like snakes."

Kwamé shushes me up. But you've heard me.

"In me locks is me power. Scooter-man, me never can lop off dese ole locks."

"Can I grow my hair like that?" I ask.

Kwamé ruffles my matted curls. "If you don't brush it from time to time," he says, "you won't have much choice!"

I swerve away and do two hard kick-offs to speed me away from Kwamé's attempts to tidy my hair.

My scooter tracks leave a white paint trail as far as the school gates. There's a whole line-up of shoe prints on the pavement with little patterns from our soles. By the thickness of the paint I reckon some kids tramped in it on purpose. It was hard to resist.

"Shoes off!" Miss Clarr shouts. "We don't want prints all over our brand new carpet on our first day."

But it's too late. My trainer prints are right there in a trail across the carpet.

"Now, what's your name?" Miss Clarr asks me.

"Lenny!"

"Well, Lenny." Miss Clarr bends down to touch the sticky footprints I've made. "Looks like you've already made your mark."

*

By the time Kwamé comes to pick me up, the smell of wet paint has gone from the crossing.

"All dry now, Scooter-man!"

You hold up your lollipop stick, Otis, and sing us across.

"I've got sunshine ...!"

"Our zebra crossing man has got some voice!" Kwamé says, and he's right.

Your song trails all down the street, up our steps, through our door and into our hall. Kwamé's still humming the sunshine song when David comes in, and he scoops me up and starts singing it too.

Over David's shoulder I watch you walk up the road with your lollipop stick. You look across and into our hall. My dads have stopped singing and you're staring at them as they kiss.

"Why is the zebra crossing man looking at you?" I ask.

Kwamé pushes the door shut with his foot.

"I think he was giving us a dirty look," he says with a sigh.

"What's a dirty look?" I ask, but no one answers. And so, like all my questions that haven't been answered, I store it up in my U.Q.B. – Unanswered Question Bank.

But I wonder –

Why would the zebra crossing man give my dads a dirty look for loving each other?

MEMORY TRACK 2

'Many Rivers To Cross'

JIMMY CLIFF

"And I can't seem to find ..."

I'm on the way back from school.

A woman in a grey Triumph Herald with silver wings – the wings belong to the car not the woman – is slowing at the crossing. She puts her head out of the window and waves to you, Otis.

"Is dat me Maeve in her ole Herald?" You tap the bonnet. "Is dat ole t'ing still sparkin' up, Maeve?"

"What a chat-up line, Otis Lawrence!" Maeve says. "It's been too long. When are you and I going to mek a likkle music again?" Maeve throws her head back and laughs. "Well, what about it?"

I watch something in your face dull, like a cloud crossing the sun.

"Otis is a ferry man now, yu know, Maeve ..." you say. "Me mus-i-shan days are well and truly over."

Kwamé's holding my hand and we're walking slowly back home. He feels in his pocket for his keys, then tells me he must have left them at the office.

"But David won't be long!" Kwamé says. "Let's sit in the sun and read while we wait."

Kwamé opens my book, but we don't get very far. Even when he sounds out the letters I still can't work out how they come from the squiggles on the page. It's so tiring and I read so slowly. I sound like a robot and I have no idea what the story's about.

So, while the story-book story goes on, I watch your real-life story, Otis. I try to work out what's going on with you and Maeve. Kwamé knows I'm not listening but he doesn't say anything because he's watching too.

Maeve parks the silver and grey car on the opposite side of the road. She walks over and throws her arms around your neck. She has a big voice like yours – a deep velvet boom – so it's not hard to hear what she says.

"One day, Otis man, you'll get that voice of yours back and when you do, you let Maeve know and we'll make some sweet music together!"

Then Maeve walks you up the road and the two of you sit side by side listening to the music that leaks out of her car windows.

Now there's no radio and it's just you two singing. And your singing is even better than the music that comes out of the radio.

You sing about wandering, about being lost, about travelling …

"*Along the white cliffs of Dover …*"

"We went to Dover," I say.

"We did!" Kwamé nods, but he's listening to the song.

Your two voices slip into smooth easy harmonies like you've sung together hundreds of times. Then you stop singing and your shoulders shake. I can see you're crying, but Kwamé hasn't noticed.

"Those two are really good together," Kwamé says. "I wonder what their story is?"

"Why is Zebra Crossing Man crying?" I ask my dad.

"Shhhh, Len," Kwamé whispers and he pretends to read the last line of my story book.

Then David arrives with the keys.

You get out of Maeve's car and walk up the street. No one answers my question, so instead of adding it to my Unanswered Question Bank I ask you.

"Zebra Crossing Man," I call out, "why are you crying?"

You bow your head.

"Lenny!" David grabs my hand, apologises to you and pulls me home.

"Why can't I ask?" I say. "First he was singing then he was crying."

"You don't ask people questions like that," David explains in a voice that I think he wants you to hear too, Otis.

But you just stand on the street and stare at me as tears track down your face. You don't try to hide them.

"Lenny … His name's Lenny?" you ask David. Your eyes are pools full of wondering.

"Yes," David mutters. "I'm so sorry about him calling out like that!"

From this day on, you call me "Lenny son".

*

In bed at night, I hear my dads listening to the song that you and Maeve sang. I hear them talking about you.

"He's not your average zebra crossing man," David says.

"And what's an average zebra crossing man like?" Kwamé asks.

"I have no idea, but in my experience they don't tend to sound like Otis Redding! He doesn't add up. Anyway, don't turn it on me. *You* were the one who said he might not approve of us."

Then the volume gets turned up so I can't hear the rest of the conversation.

"*Wandering and lost ...*"

*

This song I'm listening to now ... 'Many Rivers To Cross' by Jimmy Cliff. Every time I play it I see me and Kwamé sitting on our steps listening to you and Maeve singing like you're lost inside the song. You rocked our street as you sat in that old Herald. For the first time I felt how live music can seep deep inside you, how it can rock your world.

I take the next record out of its faded paper holder. It's lost its protective jacket. A shame – I would like to have seen what artwork was on the front.

There are so many scratches on this vinyl – more than on any other record I've played. You must have listened to this one over and over.

MEMORY TRACK 3

•

'Respect'
OTIS REDDING

I'm in Year 1. I must be about six years old.

Kwamé's in the playground too. He's talking to a teacher, making plans for the fundraising committee as usual.

Naira is with me, looking out for me like she often does.

We're playing catch, but then Naira's mum comes to collect her. Her mum waves to Kwamé so he knows she's leaving, but he doesn't respond. I carry on playing, messing around in the den at the bottom of the climbing frame. When I get bored I wander off to find Kwamé, but I can't see him anywhere.

Maybe he's gone home.

I start to walk.

As soon as I set foot out of the school gates everything feels different, like the road has got much bigger, much faster.

I know I need to turn left to get home. I put my hands up in front of me to see which hand makes the "L" for left like Kwamé showed me.

But the more I look the more I can't remember which way round an "L" goes.

And so I turn away from the school gates. The pavement goes on for ages and the houses and gardens start to blur. The wind blows and a few helicopter pods from sycamore trees twist down and land on me. I brush them off and carry on. The further I walk the taller the houses grow and I shrink and shrink till I'm a dot of a boy. Soon I'm as tiny as a helicopter pod, falling and falling to the ground to lie in the house's shadowy paths. Anyone could trample on me.

There's a hand on my back.

My heart's a drum on loudspeaker.

I don't know your name yet, but it's your hand, Otis …

"Where's your dad, Lenny son?" you ask.

Why are you calling me Lenny son? It feels weird. I'm not your son.

"*Stranger Danger!*" Miss Clarr's voice booms in my head. "*If an adult you don't know approaches you, never talk to them. If they carry on talking to you … run!*"

So I run in the opposite direction away from you. You run after me, but I'm too fast.

Now the crossing is in front of me, and beyond the crossing there's home. I can hear you shouting, yelling my name.

"Stop now, Lenny son, don't you dare cross."

Kwamé is standing at the bottom of our steps. He must be calling to me to run faster. And you're still chasing me, and you're not a stranger, but I don't know you.

"*Lenny son!*" you call.

My legs pound the crossing.

I'm in a herd of zebras bucking and leaping.

A screech of brakes.

Squeezing the breath out of me.

Hands propelling me to the other side of the road.

For a second ...

I'm flying in the air.

I'm a helicopter seed pod zooming through space.

Until ...

I land hard and scrape my arm and the side of my face.

*

On the way to the hospital you keep saying the same thing over and over.

"Him could have been dead! At least dat beast of a car drive into me leg, Lenny son, an' not your head. Just a likkle bit of road stuck in your face, no worse dan dat!"

David drives us to A&E to get the grit taken out of my face and to check out your leg.

"It not'ing," you keep saying. "Me jus' happy dat me Lenny son has only minor hinjury. We wearin' de road, Lenny son ... like it or not, we all wearin' a likkle bit of de road."

They put a few stitches in your knee where the car jammed into you, and David and Kwamé offer you a lift home.

"I'm so sorry," Kwamé says when we're squashed back in the car. "I hope you won't have to be off work."

"No, it not bad at all now de blud stop flowin' ..." you say. And then, "Today is de first time me travel in a car for long time." You shake your head like you're not enjoying the journey too much.

"You don't drive?" David asks.

"Me never learn an' now me never will."

"Never say never!" David says. "Where there's a will ..."

"Dere is no will to pump out any more poll-u-shun in the air. People all drivin' around wid so little care about de air dem breathe, an' me own lungs gettin' tight an' wheezy ..."

I see how your face is set in lines that have none of their usual joy.

"Why do you work on the crossing then?" I ask.

U.Q.B.

Awkward.

Then 'Respect' comes on the radio and interrupts the silence.

"Me band used to cover dis song," you say. "You know my namesake Otis."

You start to sing and David and Kwamé join in. They know all the words, but they can't sing it like you do. Your voice fills the car.

"What did I tell you?" David laughs at the end of the song. "Our very own Otis Redding crossing man!" Then David goes all serious. "Thank you, Otis. You saved Lenny's life."

You bump fists with Kwamé then David. I feel left out so I do the same.

We want to take you all the way home, but you insist that David drops you off at the end of your road.

"Why?" I ask when you've gone.

"I don't know," Kwamé replies. "Maybe Otis wants his privacy."

"Why?" I ask again. "He knows where *we* live."

"Perhaps it's his code of honour or something."

"What's –?"

"Oh! I don't know, Len. He's a bit of a mystery our Otis."

U.Q.B.

"What's respect?" I ask.

MEMORY TRACK 4

Jazz impro
CHARLES MINGUS

I bump fists to David at breakfast and he laughs.

Kwamé says when someone's saved your life, and hurt their own leg in the process, the proper thing to do is to make them a card.

I draw a picture of you and a picture of me on the zebra crossing ... and I give you stripes like you're an actual zebra!

In my picture I'm flying across the road like Superman without his cape.

"What have you written?" David asks.

I read it out to him.

"Thank you, Zebra Man. Sorry I made you hurt your leg. I want to sing and play in a band and never cut my hair so it grows down to the ground. Just like you. Respect from Lenny."

Then I draw a little picture of me and you – you're playing a guitar and musical notes float out of my mouth.

"Maybe you will be in a band one day," David says as he writes his translation words under mine.

"Can't Otis read?" I ask.

David laughs, but then he sees that I'm waiting for an answer.

"Not sure he'll be able to read your writing yet," he explains. "Kwamé and me are used to it, that's all."

I'm late for school because my dads wait by the wall for everyone to cross so they can give you the card when you're done. Inside they've put a voucher for The Jazz Café, the place where you told us you used to play ... so you can see whatever bands you want there. The voucher was Kwamé's idea.

David picks me up so I can hand you the card myself.

You open it and nod.

"Thought-ful an' generous an' nat at all necessary – jus' doin' me job. You should not have worried you'self about a gift ... Jus' happy me Lenny son is OK. Now let me see this art work!"

You take my card out and join fists with me.

"Respect!" I say.

"Respec', Lenny son," you say and cross us to the other side of the zebra stripes.

You sit on the wall and your locks fall forward over my card, like branches of a willow tree weeping to the ground.

MEMORY TRACK 5

'Everything's Gonna
Be Alright'
BOB MARLEY

I'm in Year 5 and we're learning about Ecology.
We have to make a sculpture out of recycled
stuff – out of anything we can find. A model out
of junk, really.

We learn how humans are ruining the Earth
by pumping so many poisons into it, like plastic
that takes 500 years to bio-degrade. (Bio-degrade
means to decompose – we're learning words like
that.) I can't believe that's true, so I look it up
and it's even worse than that. Some bottles can
take like 1,000 years … 1,000 years for just one
plastic bottle.

My head mashes up when I think about how many bottles are used in the world every day. But I try to think about it as I build my sculpture. It's not that easy to find things to use, because David keeps putting stuff in the recycle bin.

"Do we really need all this rubbish around the place?" he asks when I pile all the bits on our table.

"It's art!" I tell him. "A sculpture."

"Yes, David. It's art," Kwamé echoes, like he does when he thinks David's wrong.

I spend the whole weekend sticking bits and bobs together, painting them and adding googly eyes made of bottle tops. I think David feels bad that he called it "rubbish", so he helps me glue it together and balance it. We call it "Recycle Human" – for obvious reasons.

Over the weekend Recycle Human grows and grows until it's taller and wider than me.

Kwamé helps me carry it into school on Monday morning. Normally he doesn't walk with me any more ... I'm allowed to cross the Zebra on my own. We struggle down the hill with Recycle Human. I'm balancing the legs made from wrapping-paper tubes, and Kwamé's holding the cereal-packet head together. A trail of cornflake brains spills along the pavement as we go.

"What you got there, Lenny son?" you say with a laugh. That big deep, booming laugh always makes me feel like it's going to be a good day.

"Recycle Human."

"It so, Lenny son. It so. Recycle Hu-man ... you believe in re-hincarn-ayshun? T'ink it what we all doin', what we here for? Turnin' life over, comin' back again – you t'ink so, Lenny son? It possible?"

We're almost at school when I ask Kwamé, "Why does Otis talk like that? What does he mean?"

"Hard to know, Len. I get the feeling Otis has more than the Zebra on his mind. Our Otis is a bit of a philosopher ... One day you'll understand."

I hate it when adults say that. How will I understand if Kwamé doesn't? "What's re-hincarn-ayshun?" I ask as Kwamé drops me and Recycle Human at my classroom door.

"It's re-in-carnation – there's no 'h'." Kwamé sighs. "That's a difficult one ... ask me again later."

The U.Q.B. is full to overflowing.

*

Recycle Human gets a "good work" star, but Mr Dent doesn't choose it for the hall display. I ask him why and he says he would like to, but they're short of space.

"Perhaps you could take it home and make it to scale?" Mr Dent says. He must have seen the disappointment on my face.

"You mean shrink it?" I ask.

Mr Dent nods.

"It'll be too neat," I tell him. "I can't shrink it – that *is* the size of Recycle Human. It's like the giant mess we're making of the Earth."

I don't know why Mr Dent's laughing. I'm serious.

"I like that about you, Lenny. You know your own mind," he says, but he still sends me home with Recycle Human.

*

It's hard to carry my sculpture home on my own, but I just about manage to lug him to the crossing.

"If it isn't me Recycle Hu-man returnin' home," Otis jokes.

Its legs bash into the bollard in the middle as I walk across. I stumble and Otis catches me, but Recycle Hu-man splits apart and all the bits of him scatter over the crossing.

bottle top clothes

shoe box feet

toilet roll body

plastic lid hands

juice carton chest

"You nat to worry about a t'ing, Lenny son. Otis will gather yu Recycle Hu-man together an' you can fix him up again jus' fine, like de main man Marley sing ... *'every little t'ing gonna be alright'*. You go now an' stan' by our wall an' Otis will pick up de bits an' pieces! Don't you worry about a t'ing, Lenny son."

You ignore the beeping horns and calls for you to "Get on with it, mate". You just keep on singing and collecting up the bits of Recycle Human that have spilled all over the road.

By the time you've finished, the song's settled deep inside me.

"Every little t'ing gonna be alright ..."

MEMORY TRACK 6

'Happy Birthday'
STEVIE WONDER

It's my 11th birthday. My present stands propped up against the kitchen table.

My dads have wrapped its curves in newspaper and tied it with a big red bow, but the tell-tale neck sticks out.

I untie the ribbon, rip the paper open and un-zip the soft case.

I'm holding my breath.

Could it be?

My own guitar.

My first ever guitar. My best present ever.

I carry it into school on my back like a trophy.

"What you got dere, Lenny son?" you say. "Only de best t'ing man can carry on his back, a shell … fe protect-shun an' power! You have music anywhere you waan to go now an' who know where it will tek you. Music fe whatever crossin' you gwaan make. Now music it somet'ing Otis can learn you. Me will hintroduce you to me forever songs fe you to play."

"One day," I say, "but I can't read music yet."

"It nat de only way … Jus' listen up an' let the rhythm play thru you … let dat music call an' you respond, Lenny son. It how me learn."

*

All that summer holidays I did exactly what you said.

Listened, sang and learned by ear to play, listened, sang and learned by ear to play.

By the time I tried to read a page of music the notes had already hatched from tadpoles darting around a page. I could play the song over and over and match the note on the page to the note in my ear. Otis was right. It was a good way to learn.

There was never anything boring, never anything *just* black and white about music to me.

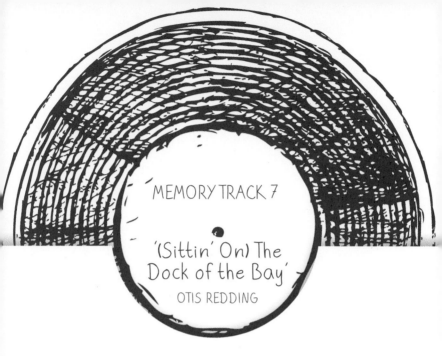

MEMORY TRACK 7

'(Sittin' On) The Dock of the Bay'
OTIS REDDING

We bump respect fists at the crossing like always.

Then I get the feeling you're testing me.

You sing, "*Sittin' on the dock ...*"

I sing, "*Watching the tide ...!*"

And that's how we carry on till the end of the song, with harmonies and everything. Our voices sound good together until you break out into a cough.

"Nice, Lenny son. Very nice!" You splutter as you cough. "Me swear all dese dyam fumes are mekin' me short of breat'. Dis be not'ing like de fresh breeze me used to breathe when me was a boy, but one day I will breathe easy again … Meantime sharing me songs meks me feel de sea breeze in me soul, Lenny son. De sea breeze in me soul."

And I'm carried on the waves of your encouraging words all through that first day of secondary school.

MEMORY TRACK 8

●

'Everybody Hurts'
R.E.M.

Year 10. I was 15 years old.

It was the day my girlfriend Joss split up with me.

When I listen now to track 8, I can't believe how it makes me feel. I thought I'd got over Joss, but then like Otis said ...

"You don't get over people, you jus' have to accep' dem not in your life no more an' anyways, Lenny son, tek it from me, you never dyam forget a first love. It sweet as sugar cane an' painful as hell fire."

Now David knocks at my door, comes in and rests the guitar against the wall.

"That's two hours. Good going, Len. I still don't know how you can focus with music on, but ..." David puts a cup of tea and a plate of biscuits next to my laptop. "Seems like you're getting on with it."

I wipe my eyes. I can't believe I'm tearing up remembering Joss.

"Thanks, Dad," I mumble.

"You OK?"

I nod to get David to leave my room, but I'm not really OK. I feel like I'm Lost in Memory Land. I take the needle off the record and it stops dead. It's how it felt between me and Joss. I've got to try to put some theory around all these memories or I'll drown in them.

I go online to find the only video clip I've ever found of you. There you are, Otis ...

I look closer and I notice for the first time that the skinny love-struck girl with red lips, a beehive and black boots singing at your side is Maeve. I turn up the volume.

It's 'The Harder They Come, The Harder They Fall' – Jimmy Cliff.

Why would you give up on all this, Otis?

You weren't happy when I asked you that question. You met it with a silence as deep as a canyon. Another Otis question for the Unanswered Question Bank.

MEMORY TRACK 9

'Sorry'
TRACY CHAPMAN

Year 11. Just before GCSEs.

I'm late for an exam and I bowl straight over the road. I don't wait for you to do our "respec' fist ferry man t'ing".

"You t'ink you're growin' to a big man, but you don't hunderstand a t'ing, Lenny son ... not about me ... not about me life. Not about why man can sing sometime an' why him lose de joy in performin'."

It's the first time you've ever been angry with me and it hurts because I don't understand.

But even in anger, your voice is weak like the colour has drained out of it and you struggle to catch your breath.

At school, I worry about you, about the coughing and the wheezing. And about why you're getting so angry.

But then, on the way home, you have a song ready for me. It's 'Sorry' by Tracy Chapman and you sing it so well that I forget to say what I've been thinking all day – that a doctor should check out your asthma.

Kwamé tells me this 'Sorry' song used to be played everywhere.

"It's actually called 'Baby Can I Hold You'," he says, "but no one ever thinks of it as that."

Whatever it's called, I like Tracy Chapman's voice – it's so mellow, but so full of hurt. It makes me think of Otis.

"Words don't come easily ..."

I try to sing but the words come out all broken ...

... Broken love ... broken words.

MEMORY TRACK 10

'Father and Son'
CAT STEVENS
(YUSUF ISLAM)

A Level Psychology Exam – Take 1.

You were talking in songs, but I could tell you weren't happy when you lost it with me that time.

I promised you I'd never smoke, not ever, but you caught me with a cigarette in hand.

"One smoke is one smoke too many, an' I wish me never took dat poison to me mouth ..."

I thought I could divert you by asking about your asthma, but the lecture you gave me made me wish I hadn't bothered.

"Joss used to use an inhaler," I tried as a gentle way to raise the subject.

"The day me use an hinhaler is the day me leave dis road," you said. "No question, Lenny son, no hinhaler for me. Me will just keep on singin' to open up dese ole lungs. Promise me, Lenny son. Dat is de last poison-stick you smoke."

And it was.

As I look back now, with behind sight, I knew life was going wrong for you. Should I have said something to Kwamé and David? Maybe if I had ...

"You can't learn psychology from a book, Lenny son. But you can learn it from dis road." That's what you tell me on the day of my exam. I know you're just being kind – calming my nerves.

Then, on the way home I'm so fed up. I know I've messed it up.

I walk out into the road and put my hand out for a car to stop, but you yell me down, your voice like an alarm. You wave your lollipop stick around and I think, 'Otis isn't well – he's not behaving right.'

But instead of speaking out I get embarrassed that you've shamed me up on the road.

I think, 'Who are you to treat me like a kid – shout at me, lecture me, call me *Lenny son*?'

"What you t'inkin', big man?" you say. "You t'ink you too dyam big to be mashed into the ground? Lenny son ..."

You get right up in my face and point at me. It makes me want to jab back.

"Remember I have save you an' your Recycle Hu-man. Don't mek me have to pick dem bits of yu off a dis road. Nearly happen once before. Remember? Maybe a cat got nine lives, but you a hu-man, Lenny son. Me nah waan to be recylin' yu."

"I don't need you to cross me any more, Otis," I snap like a spoiled kid. "And I'm not your *Lenny son*!"

I'm sorry ... I want to say it over and over.

You look at me. You're a broken man. You're as fragile as Recycle Hu-man and about to crumple into bits like him. You stagger over to our wall and sit down.

"No song today, Otis?" I can see how tired you are.

"Sometime a man don't feel like singin' … If you care fe how me feel you can go an' look up 'Father and Son' by Cat Stevens. Dat a song fe we now – I t'ink him gwaan change him name to Yusuf Islam. Him not a cat no more …"

I check to see if you're joking, but there's no smile on your face. Not for the first time, I think your Otis philosophy isn't clear as it used to be.

A ginger cat walks along our wall and you put your hand out to stroke it, so gentle it's like you're comforting it.

"You is lucky yu know, likkle Tom, fe you have nine whole lives to live."

*

In my room I look up 'Father and Son'. I half expect the song not to exist … the way you talk it's hard to know for sure what's in your mind.

The song's a dad singing his thoughts to his son and a son singing his thoughts back to his dad. It's about pulling away from childish days …

childish ways. It makes me really sad. Not just for you, Otis, but for David and Kwamé and me too.

But then I think about how I like the way the song's structured, so it's the father's words and then the son's. They're taking it in turns, so it's a proper conversation-song. I might try writing something like this. All the things you want to say, but can't …

Maybe it's something like I'm trying to do now, with sharing memory tracks with you, Otis.

I play 'Father and Son' over and over. I listen to the music, to the father's lyrics and the son's. I listen to them reaching to understand each other as I try to work out why you're so sad.

*

I look for you before and after school. I want to tell you how much I liked that song … how much I got it.

But it's not until a week later that you're back. I don't have a lesson, but I wait till you've finished on the crossing, then I walk up the road to meet you, guitar on my back.

You have deep dark rings under your eyes.

We sit on our wall for a bit and you don't seem to want to talk, so I play 'Father and Son'. You sing the father part and I sing the son.

I don't think we've ever sung together like that ... not so we get lost in it, not so we're two musicians inside the music.

We're in the song, me and you. So we don't see the people on the other side of the crossing who've stopped to listen. We don't see Kwamé and David on the steps of our flat. When we finish, they clap and wipe at their teary eyes.

You ignore them, squeeze my arm and stand up.

"It not easy all right. But you're on your way now, Lenny son. You nat need old Otis no more."

The day you lost it

It's just before the Easter holidays. I come out of college and you're standing a few steps into the crossing, not even on the island in the middle. You're holding a little kid in your arms and you won't let him go. A child's red cap is lying on the road.

I can hear your breath, heavy and wheezing like an old engine.

A crowd has gathered and a mum is talking to you. Her voice is like you've taken her child hostage, like she's trying to persuade you to release him. But you refuse and she starts to scream.

"Let him go!" the woman screams over and over. "He wasn't in any danger ... I was holding his hand. Look – he just dropped his cap."

You're jabbing your finger at the woman.

"You should hold his hand fe dear life ..." You splutter and cough out the words. "You know how dear dis life is?"

Otis ... I can see you're holding the little boy too tight. You're squeezing the breath out of him. His eyes are wide and shoot out sparks of terror.

"How soft is him hand," you say, almost to yourself now. "You mus' hold him so much tighter ... An' if he runs back an' get him cap an' a car come smashin' in to him ... what will you say den? You gwaan set di blame on me. I know you gwaan blame me. You have always blame me, Honor, why you can never forgive me? Now it your turn to feel what it like. You gotta pay close attention, dis dear life can go in an hinstant ... *Whoosh* and it lost for ever, you nat remember, Honor?" Then you cradle the boy even tighter, like he's a baby, like he's your baby. "No cry, my Lenny son. No cry."

The boy is frozen with fear in your arms.

"I'm not Honor!" the mother yells. Then, "It's all right, Jaky. It's going to be all right."

"Call the police!" someone shouts. "Call the police ... the man's lost it."

"It all right, my Lenny son, Otis done save you, Otis mek sure you have safe crossin'. You not gonna leave Otis again. You not gonna cross into heaven, me don't believe in Honor's heaven, not dis time, me son, me caan't stan' it again. An' all dese year I no see de truth. You been waitin' fe me to save you on de crossin' ... comin' back year after year ... recycle hu-man, a new Lenny, a second chance fe Otis to save you now, me likkle Lenny son."

You're on your knees, collapsed and sobbing and struggling to catch your breath.

"Someone get help!" the mother shouts. "Please! The man's struggling to breathe!"

I walk up to you and reach out. I make my voice quiet and soft like I'm talking to a child.

"His name's not Lenny, Otis. *I'm* Lenny!" I say. "Otis, please let him go. You're scaring him and you're not well."

Now I'm close I can see your eyes. They're glazed over and watery with confusion. But I hold your face in my hand and force you to see me and something in your eyes shifts.

"Otis ... *I'm* Lenny, remember?"

You shake your head over and over and cry like I have never seen anyone cry before, like your insides are ripping apart and spilling onto the crossing. I hold you tight to stop you exploding in sadness.

"You nat me Lenny son, now me see de truth," you sob. "No matter how much me want you to be ... an' now you is gettin' ready to leave me."

You look down at the boy and up at me and clamp your hands over your ears as the sirens get closer and louder.

I take the boy and hand him over to his mum.

"Stop dat Babylon song, blasting me ears," you gasp. "No siren. Shut di racket up!"

When they see it's a wheezing, broken-down Otis on the crossing, the police cars switch off their sirens and move people away from the road.

You lie on the crossing, face down, locks flowing, arms outstretched as you weep into the white stripe on the road.

"No handcuffs," a police officer says, as he carefully lifts you up. You don't resist.

"And you are?" the officer asks me. "Any relation?"

"Him nat me son!" you say.

"No, but I am your friend … Otis is my friend," I tell the officer.

Afterwards

Kwamé and David call the station and we go down there together, but as we're not Otis's family the police won't tell us anything.

A week later I find your record player in the hall and your vinyl stacked next to it. Kwamé said you refused to come in. You just wanted me to have the player and your old records, and you left a card with your email and address. Not even any words written to me, only what you told Kwamé to pass on. You were moving to St Lucia to stay with your sister and breathe the sea breeze. We had an open invite to visit anytime.

No explanation. Nothing. So now I'm asking ...

*

I pause before I press "send".

What if this upsets Otis more?

What if it's better for him to walk away and cut all ties?

Then I think of all the times we spent together … and it feels like it's worth sending him these memory tracks.

Sending them to see if anything comes back to answer all these unanswered questions.

I press "send" before I can change my mind.

*

I can't take it back now. And I don't want to. The words have flown out of me, and something's shifted.

Maybe I can do this.

I open my revision notes again and start on the theory section. Mrs Wei's right … it makes better sense when you care.

FUTURE SINGLE

'Ferry Man'
OTIS LINDEN LAWRENCE
& LENNY MARLON

I hear nothing from Otis.

And the longer I don't hear from him the more I wish I hadn't sent my email – except that now I've been able to focus on my revision much better. But what if I never hear from him again?

Then, on the morning of my Psychology exam, this enters my inbox.

Dear Lenny Son,

My sister, Lorraine, read me what you sent – at least she tried to read it, but she got so emotional she had to take her time. I got emotional too, for so many reasons.

It's Lorraine who is writing this for me. I want to be honest and tell you something I've kept hidden all my life.

I can hardly read or write. Sorry I couldn't leave any words for you when I left. I couldn't write this letter without Lorraine. I can't read music either, but that never hampered me half as much as not being able to read words. If you wonder why none of this is in my voice, then ask Lorraine. She refuses to write how I speak. She says it's not the English of the Queen!

Thanks for sending me your news and your Memory Tracks. I have plenty of my own to add when you come and see me.

So many things I want to talk about with you more.

The sun is shining here and I'm sitting on the dock of the bay all day!

Lorraine is looking after me, bossing me around, making me use a damn inhaler. The sea breeze is helping my lungs too. (She just cuffed me over the head for saying how bossy she is – so that is proof!)

The "Realisation" – that's what Lorraine calls that day – feels like a long time ago now. When I read your telling of it, I can't believe it happened – that it was me there on the crossing with all that going on in my head.

Lorraine thinks I should explain some things to you. She thinks it's always been my problem – that I don't let people in. She said I should tell you what happened that day and *why* it happened. It might send you to look over some of them memories again and help you understand something about Otis Linden Lawrence, make you see the "Realisation" in some other ways.

Stick with that inner scribe, Lenny man. It's a powerful instrument you have there, if I remember it after all this time.

I like the song you put out on SoundCloud ... very lyrical, sweet-smooth. I like these lines the best.

"All those lines in-printed on my mind
And no matter what you might say
The road has soul
The road is singing ..."

And it seems like *you* got lost a little too in Naira's gold-green eyes!

But I am sorry for not replying sooner. I didn't know what to say, but I hope my Ferry Man thoughts can start to answer your questions. Maybe you and I will "unscramble" some of this, as you say, and write it as a song one day.

Maybe we will sing it as a soul song together ... like a father and a son in

spirit – now that I know you're not my
Lenny son.

I have started singing a bit again. Would
you believe – Maeve's been visiting family
here and we've sung a couple of times
at the bar at the end of our road! That
woman sure doesn't give up!

Ferry Man

Long, long time ago
Another world away
I had a son, you see
Another Lenny
He was my son
Long, long time ago
He was making a crossing

While I was busy chatting

Just a normal day you see
Sun was shining
Birds were singing
You know the road
You know the place in the road

Lenny son
No crossing in those days
They painted it in
After the blood was spilled
Black and white lines

It was me to blame you see
I let go of his hand

That is why
I stopped my singing
I stopped my band

You know the place in the road
The crossing
Just a normal day
You would say
Until it ended

He dropped his toy
Ran into that road
Pulled his hand from my hand
Before I could catch him
He was under them wheels
Crumpled
I held him in my arms
My beautiful Lenny son
My boy

Everything was broken,
All gone
My Honor, his mother, gone from me too ...
in time
All honour gone
And nothing but blame' where lovin' used to
be

Time passed and they built a crossing there
I became the ferry man
For years and years and years
Saving other people's children

Maeve told me that Honor was to marry
again
Start a new family
I was a broken man
Then I walked past your door and heard
your name
I thought it was a sign
For me to stay
As soon as I heard your name
I felt such pain
Then I pulled myself together and I thought
to myself
No Otis Man
Don't give up

Here is a sign
Here is your Lenny singing to you from the
road
To stay close
Here he is come back to sing you his soul
song

Then you got all grown up
I couldn't stand the idea you too would go
away

Then comes one day
Out of the blue you would say
Busy, busy roads to cross
It all got too damn busy in my mind
You were right
I wasn't well
I couldn't breathe
My head was playing tricks on me
Spun me right back in time
To the soft skull of Lenny's head
His soft curls
His red cap

I scooped that boy up and held him in my
arms
And I could not let him go
Would not let him go

I never heard the mother shout at me
I never heard the boy crying
I never hear the police siren
Until I saw you in the road and all the years
slipped by me
And I knew it was time to go away
Just like the song cat say.

Now, Lenny, you go focus on your Psychology exam. Don't you dare tell me you don't have the "capacity" – there's plenty of capacity in that head of yours. You show them, Lenny. Write that essay on memory now. Write the words for me, for Otis.

I'm learning those words too – Lorraine's teaching me to read and write. And compared to my Lorraine, you've got nothing to complain about in that Mrs Wei. My sister is one tough teacher!

Memory is a mighty complicated thing to put into words. The thing to remember is it's never the same with any two people, never the same, Lenny son.

One Love ... maybe ... but many truths.

Your good friend,
Otis (Ferry Man) Lawrence

P.S. Has it rained there yet? I swear it was all that dry road dust that got into my lungs. I hope to see you in the St Lucia sunshine sometime soon.

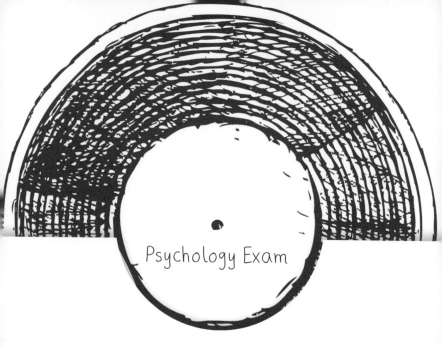

Psychology Exam

I sit in the hall, legs fidgeting under the tiny table.

I don't fit here any more.

Exam question.

Choose 1 question below ... and write an essay on memory. Give examples to illustrate your understanding of the theory.

The words fly from my pen ...

Otis was the zebra crossing man on our street. I've known him for 15 years – since I was four.

You wouldn't think you could learn so much from just crossing backwards and forwards over a road. Maybe some people would assume you couldn't learn very much from someone who can hardly write or read. But Otis is one of the best teachers I have ever known. He taught me how to think, he taught me about life, and he taught me how to write songs.

In this essay I'm looking at 'episodic memory' – episodes in your life you'll never forget.

Like the first day of school, and the day Otis saved my life, and the day I discovered how complex memory is. I didn't learn from a text book, but from all Otis taught me ... of how music and memory flow together like water flowing into one river.

*

Long goodbyes to Kwamé and David are over. And yes, Dads, for the 100th time I *have* got my passport!

Rucksack on back.

Guitar slung across my back. My trophy and my shell.

I walk up the road and sit on our wall for a moment. I wonder what it will be like to chat to Otis somewhere other than this wall. I look up at the sky and see clouds scudding by so fast it's like they're sprinting after each other.

"Life is not'ing like a sprint, son! Faster you learn that, faster you start winnin'."

I feel the first heavy raindrop land on my head, staccato rain. First minims, then quavers, and now a full-blown band of deafening, drenching rain.

"*Yu call dis rain? Yu should see it back home when de rains come.*"

"What are you doing sitting there, Len? Get under this!"

The rain streams so hard over my face I have to wipe it away to see who's there.

"What happened? Lost your super-recogniser powers?"

"Naira!" I laugh. "Don't think I ever had any. You made that up!"

"I didn't!" She laughs too, and holds a big black umbrella over my head. "Get under. You'll ruin your guitar."

"It's got a hard cover!"

"*It* might have, but you haven't. You're soaked."

Under the shell of her umbrella we're up close, and I can see how different she looks without her police uniform. Younger, more like the Naira I used to know.

"But I'm crossing here," I tell her.

"What's wrong with the Pelican?" she asks, as rain streams over the edges of her umbrella.

"It's not the Zebra, is it?" I say.

"True!" Naira says. "Poor old Otis. A lot of memories on that crossing. I wonder what happened to him?" She looks at the road and then back at me. "But check all that rain."

"*Many rivers to cross!*" I sing.

"Let's just get across alive!" Naira says.

It's not her fault. She doesn't know, but somewhere deep in my soul I feel how Otis must have felt to make all those crossings. I pretend it's the driving rain I'm wiping from my eyes.

We're hovering on the kerb. A car, its windscreen wipers racing to keep up with the rain, slows to let us cross. I look into Naira's gold-green eyes and link my arm in hers. We cross together, one last time, for Otis's sake, like we used to when we were kids.

Our books are tested
for children and young people by
children and young people.

Thanks to everyone who consulted on
a manuscript for their time and effort in
helping us to make our books better
for our readers.